TH[illegible]
OF VERY DISGUSTING
MONSTERS IN IT!

Hairy ones, smelly ones, fat ones, oozy ones. None of them are very nice, and they study the Monsterbook to become more not very nice.

Monsterbook is written by monsters, for monsters. A filthy, fact-packed handbook to everything monster!

Michael Broad spent much of his childhood gazing out of the window imagining he was somewhere more interesting. Now he's a grown-up, Michael still spends a lot of time gazing out of the window imagining he's somewhere more interesting – but these days he writes and illustrates books as well.

michaelbroad.co.uk

Books by Michael Broad

MONSTERBOOK: PONGDOLLOP AND THE SCHOOL STINK

MONSTERBOOK: SNOTGOBBLE AND THE BOGEY BULLY

MONSTERBOOK: LUMPYDUMP AND THE TERROR TEACHER

MONSTERBOOK: RUMBLEFART AND THE BEASTLY BOTTOM

JAKE CAKE: THE FOOTBALL BEAST

JAKE CAKE: THE PIRATE CURSE

JAKE CAKE: THE ROBOT DINNER LADY

JAKE CAKE: THE SCHOOL DRAGON

JAKE CAKE: THE VISITING VAMPIRE

JAKE CAKE: THE WEREWOLF TEACHER

MONSTERBOOK
Rumblefart
and the
Beastly Bottom
MICHAEL BROAD

PUFFIN

For David (the cake monster)

PUFFIN BOOKS

Published by the Penguin Group
Penguin Books Ltd, 80 Strand, London WC2R 0RL, England
Penguin Group (USA) Inc., 375 Hudson Street, New York, New York 10014, USA
Penguin Group (Canada), 90 Eglinton Avenue East, Suite 700, Toronto, Ontario, Canada M4P 2Y3 (a division of Pearson Penguin Canada Inc.)
Penguin Ireland, 25 St Stephen's Green, Dublin 2, Ireland (a division of Penguin Books Ltd)
Penguin Group (Australia), 250 Camberwell Road, Camberwell, Victoria 3124, Australia (a division of Pearson Australia Group Pty Ltd)
Penguin Books India Pvt Ltd, 11 Community Centre, Panchsheel Park, New Delhi – 110 017, India
Penguin Group (NZ), 67 Apollo Drive, Rosedale, North Shore 0632, New Zealand (a division of Pearson New Zealand Ltd)
Penguin Books (South Africa) (Pty) Ltd, 24 Sturdee Avenue, Rosebank, Johannesburg 2196, South Africa

Penguin Books Ltd, Registered Offices: 80 Strand, London WC2R 0RL, England

puffinbooks.com

First published 2010
1

Set in Perpetua
Made and printed in England by Clays Ltd, St Ives plc

British Library Cataloguing in Publication Data
A CIP catalogue record for this book is available from the British Library

ISBN: 978–0–141–32653–5

www.greenpenguin.co.uk

CONTENTS

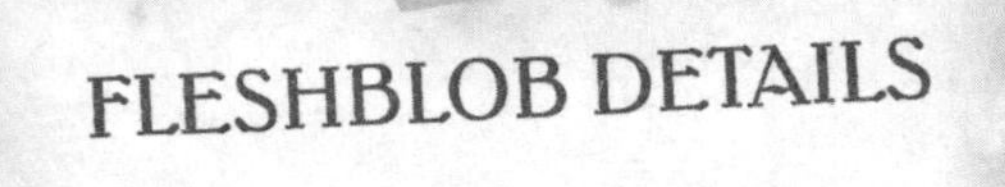

NAME ......Will......

ADDRESS 33 Highland Road

this book belongs to URK
MONSTERBOOK
WELCOME TO THE REVOLTING WORLD OF THE MONSTERBOOK! THE GRISLY GUIDE TO ALL THINGS MONSTER!
Whether you're hideously hairy, terrifyingly tentacled, creepily clawed or just a great big mess of disgustingness, Monsterbook has everything you need for a career in fear.
This book comes with the name and address of your allocated fleshblob FOR SCARE-TRAINING PURPOSES!

THIS IS URK

Urk is a monster.
But to his parents' disappointment he's not very scary.

When Urk began scare training with the MONSTERBOOK he made friends with Will, his allocated fleshblob!

THIS IS WILL

Will is a human.
He thinks monsters are revolting, but also very interesting.

SCARE TRAINING

When Urk's meant to be out scaring Will, the pair watch TV, eat snacks and read the MONSTERBOOK.
Urk makes up weekly scare reports for his parents, and Will learns more about the disgusting world of Monsterland.

MONSTERLAND

Monsterland is the underground world where monsters live. It's very dirty, smelly and lit by thousands of stolen light bulbs.

Earthy tunnels lead to the human world above, where monsters enter through secret doorways - hidden under beds, behind curtains and inside wardrobes...

1

Miffni and the Stink Storm

With the *Monsterbook* tucked safely in his rucksack, Urk crept down the murky brown hallway and held his breath as he passed his sister's bedroom. It was a scare-training night in Monsterland and the young monster was looking forward to seeing his fleshblob friend Will, so he didn't want any trouble from Miffni.

Unlike her brother, Miffni was huge

and scary and loved causing trouble, and to make matters worse her best friend Pong Pong was staying for a sleepover. Pong Pong was just as mean as Miffni, and Urk had learned to stay out of their way.

'WHEN THEY SEE US THEY'LL SCREAM AND SCREAM!' boomed Miffni, from inside her room.

'AND MAYBE THEY'LL DO A LITTLE WEE WEE TOO!' boomed Pong Pong.

This was followed by shrieks of snorting laughter that made the door rattle on its hinges. Urk froze like a statue in the hallway, but it wasn't fear that had stopped him in his tracks – it was his brotherly duty to spy on his sister.

The mention of screams and wee

wee meant Miffni and Pong Pong were planning to frighten some fleshblobs, because a wet mattress is a very high achievement for a monster. But his sister was too young to go scare training in the world of humans and Urk hoped to hear something he could use against her.

As the laughter died down, the young

monster crept forward and pressed his ear against the wood. He could hear the pair whispering to each other, but couldn't make out exactly what they were saying.

Then the voices suddenly hushed.

Uh oh! thought Urk, as a thunder of footfalls rattled the floorboards and shook the walls, and before he could move away from it the door flew open.

'CAUGHT YA!' growled Miffni, filling half of the doorway.

The other half of the doorway was filled with Pong Pong, who was thinner than her friend, but had much bigger hair-bunches and triple-lens spectacles perched on her snout.

Urk peered up at the glaring monsters and tried to think of a good reason for snooping. When this failed he decided to make a run for it, but only got a short way down the hall before a long stripy

tentacle hooked the straps of his rucksack and lifted him off the ground.

'Not so fast, you little Bugwart!' said Pong Pong, flexing her extendable tentacle until he

swung round to face them. 'We have a few questions for you.'

'What did you hear?' demanded Miffni.

'Er, n-nothing,' Urk stammered. 'Something about wee wee?'

'Nothing else?' said Pong Pong, shaking him up and down.

'No!' snapped Urk, squirming to pull himself free. 'Now let me go!'

Pong Pong looked to Miffni, who shrugged and nodded.

The tentacle immediately released the rucksack, causing Urk to tumble to the floor. The young monster picked himself up and was about to turn away from the sniggering pair when Miffni spoke again.

'Did you pack an umbrella?' she asked, ducking into her room and returning with a steaming, stinking litterbin. The basket overflowed with rubbish, rotten fruit and empty snail shells. 'Because I've heard there's a storm coming.'

'What storm?' Urk asked suspiciously, slowly backing away.

'A STINK STORM!' roared Miffni and Pong Pong together, grabbing clumps of the smelly rubbish and pelting them at him. Knowing the young monster liked to stay tidy and didn't enjoy foul smells, they shrieked with laughter as the filth flew through the air.

Urk charged towards the front door as the mucky mounds thudded all around him. Some hit his rucksack, but most of them missed as he ducked and dived through the shower of litter. Once outside he raced down the stairwells of Terror Towers, dashed through the alleyways and didn't look back until he reached the edge of Monster City.

The young monster slowed to a walk as he made his way though the earthy tunnels leading out of Monsterland, where he flicked empty snail shells off his fur and pulled wads of sticky paper from his rucksack. Urk was still wondering what Miffni and Pong Pong were planning when he plucked a large ball of screwed-up paper from his shoulder and unfolded it.

The tunnels were dark, so Urk paused beneath a grubby light bulb to read it.

'Uh oh!' he said aloud.

2

What's a Squidlet?

'BOO!' said Urk, jumping from the wardrobe in his friend's bedroom and pulling the rucksack off his shoulders. The young monster quickly checked the bag for slime and snail shells and then

dumped it on Will's desk.

'ARGH!' said Will. 'What's up?'

'We have a bit of a problem,' Urk replied, taking out the ball of crumpled paper. 'Which means instead of watching TV tonight, we're going to have to make another trip to Monsterland.'

'I don't think I can go tonight!' said Will, grabbing a poster from his desk and holding it up. 'I have to learn my lines for

this dumb school play tomorrow. I was going to ask you to help me with it.'

Urk looked at the poster advertising *Beauty and the Beast* at Will's school the following evening, and then unfolded the sticky ball of paper from the stink storm. Aside from the creases and stains and blobs of goo, the posters were identical.

'Where did you get that?' gasped Will.

'My sister had it,' said Urk, screwing the poster back into a ball. 'She's planning a fleshblob scare with her horrible Squidlet friend Pong Pong. And it looks like your school play is their target.'

'But everyone's parents will be there!' said Will.

Urk nodded gravely.

'What's a Squidlet?' asked Will.

'A squidgy monster from Snotshire,' said Urk, pulling out the *Monsterbook* and flicking through the 'Gruesome Gallery', which contained all known monsters. When he found the Squidlet entry, he placed the book on the desk for his friend to read.

SQUIDLET

Squidlets are tall, slimy monsters from the Snotshire countryside in the outer regions of Monsterland.
They have a very sensitive snout for sniffing out Gobblers to eat, and use their extendable tentacle to pluck them from their deep earthy burrows.

Squidlets are not terribly bright.

GOBBLER

Gobblers are the largest, fattest slugs in Monsterland who were awarded monster status due to their incredible size and revolting appearance.

Unfortunately for Gobblers, their pus-warts make them very tasty so they have to burrow deep underground to avoid becoming lunch.

'So what are Miffni and Pong Pong planning to do exactly?' asked Will, closing the book. 'Because if they intend to steal all the chairs or something like that, and the school have to cancel the play, then that wouldn't exactly be a *bad* thing . . .'

'They mentioned screaming and wee wee,' said Urk.

'Oh,' said Will, clearly disappointed. 'Then what should we do?'

'Well, if we can find out exactly what

they're planning,' said Urk, packing the *Monsterbook* away, 'I think telling my mum and dad should be enough to put a stop to it. Miffni hasn't even finished Basic Boo, so she's not allowed to go on scare manoeuvres.'

BASIC BOO

Monsterland's junior fright school where little monsters learn ugly faces, grisly groans and creepy noises.

'But if your sister hasn't finished the basics, how could she mastermind a big scare?' asked Will.

'I don't know,' Urk replied thoughtfully, as if this had been bothering him too. 'Because she's also really lazy, and has never shown an interest in scaring fleshblobs before.'

'Maybe her friend is the brains behind it?' suggested Will.

'Pong Pong?' Urk gasped. 'Not likely, she's as thick as slug jelly!'

SLUG JELLY

Monster pudding made from jellied slugs and eyeballs.

'Well, if we're going to find out we'd better get a move on,' said Will, pulling a sheet of dirty sackcloth over his head and poking two forks through the material. The disguise made him look like a Jub Jub – a monster so disgusting it has to stay covered at all times. This allowed Will

to walk freely in Monsterland without getting squashed or eaten.

Urk and Will stepped into the wardrobe, moved through the hidden doorway and headed down the damp, smelly tunnels leading to Monsterland. Several monsters were trudging up the tunnels for a night of frights in children's bedrooms – including a Snooper, a Gum Gum and an Ooof. Will remembered these strange creatures from the *Monsterbook* and chuckled to himself. Later they passed a nasty-looking Snaggler, reminding Will how lucky he was to have Urk looking out for him.

SNOOPER

Snoopers are long-nosed monsters that hop around children's bedrooms looking for foul things to smell, like dirty socks and smelly shoes. They are totally harmless and not even scary to look at.

GUM GUM

Gum Gums leave pink gummy deposits on the carpets in fleshblob homes. They are impossible to remove and usually result in parents banning their children from eating bubblegum.

OOOF

Ooofs are very stupid monsters that rummage in school bags and eat paper with writing on it believing this will make them clever. An adult Ooof can eat between two and three homework books a night.

SNAGGLER

Snagglers specialize in tangling children's hair while they sleep, spending many hours tying complicated knots and back-combing large matted clumps with a fine-toothed fingernail.

3

A Huge Thud

'So what part are you playing in *Beauty and the Beast*?' asked Urk, as they left the tunnels and stepped into the murky world of Monsterland. Thousands of light bulbs buzzed angrily in the damp ceiling

of the cavern, shining over the sprawling dungheap that was Monster City.

'I'm playing tree number two,' said Will.

'You're playing a tree?' chuckled Urk.

Will nodded awkwardly.

'And the tree has lines to learn?' Urk smiled.

'I'm supposed to say "RUSTLE! RUSTLE!" when the beast appears.'

'And you need help to remember that?' Urk frowned.

'I know the lines, I just keep forgetting to say it in rehearsals,' said Will. 'Grant Butcher, who's playing the part of the beast, keeps putting me off. And when Miss Star isn't looking he pushes me over.'

'Who's Miss Star?' asked Urk.

'Oh, she's our new drama teacher,'

explained Will. 'We have a new one every year because they all quit during the school play. That's why I left my lines until the last minute, hoping Miss Star would quit too. But she stuck with it and now it looks like I'll have to go on stage!'

'We'll worry about that later,' said Urk, patting his friend on the shoulder. 'And

maybe Miffni and Pong Pong *will* steal the chairs, and the school will have to cancel the play after all.'

'I wish!' said Will.

The pair laughed as they entered Monster City and made their way through the backstreets and alleyways until they reached the block of mud flats where Urk's family lived.

'Now, we'll have to be really quiet when we go in,' said Urk, as they approached the main doors of Terror Towers. 'And hopefully we can spy on my sister without her even knowing we're there.'

'I'll be as quiet as a m–' Will began, but stopped when Urk suddenly shrieked and bundled them both into a nearby bush. The young monster quickly clasped

his hand over an area of sack where he guessed Will's mouth was.

'They're coming!' Urk whispered urgently.

Moments later the doors flew open with an enormous *bang!* and Miffni and Pong Pong stomped and slithered from the building, chatting and giggling

loudly as they headed into the maze of alleyways.

'Phew!' sighed Urk. 'That was close!'

'Mmf mmf mm!' replied Will.

'Oh, sorry!' said Urk, taking his hand away and helping his friend to his feet.

'Where do you think they're going?' asked Will, dusting himself off.

'I don't know,' said Urk, peering down

the long dark alley to see Miffni and Pong Pong taking a right turn. 'We'd better follow them and try to get close enough to hear what they're saying.'

Urk and Will followed Miffni and Pong Pong as they zigzagged through the maze of gloomy backstreets, keeping out of sight and listening to their chatter. Fortunately Urk's sister and her friend had very loud voices, but all they spoke about was different flavours of lipgloss, including Rotten Raspberry and Fizzy Fish Guts.

'I still don't understand how these two could possibly mastermind a big scare,' whispered Urk, dropping back to a safe distance as they took a left turn into Monster City High Street.

'It does seem very unlikely,' agreed Will.

Hanging back, they tracked the two pairs of hair-bunches bobbing down the High Street above the heads of smaller monsters and ducked into a doorway when Miffni and Pong Pong stopped to cross the road.

'They're heading for The Monster Mash!' said Urk, watching as the two monsters skipped arm in arm towards

a large building that had a fat lumpy monster guarding the entrance. 'It's a youth club for teenage monsters.'

'Who's the big blob?' asked Will, pointing at the huge creature blocking the doors.

'I think it's a Thud,' said Urk, taking out the *Monsterbook* and flicking through its pages until he found the entry for a Thud. 'Yeah, here it is. Not one to be messed with by the looks of it.'

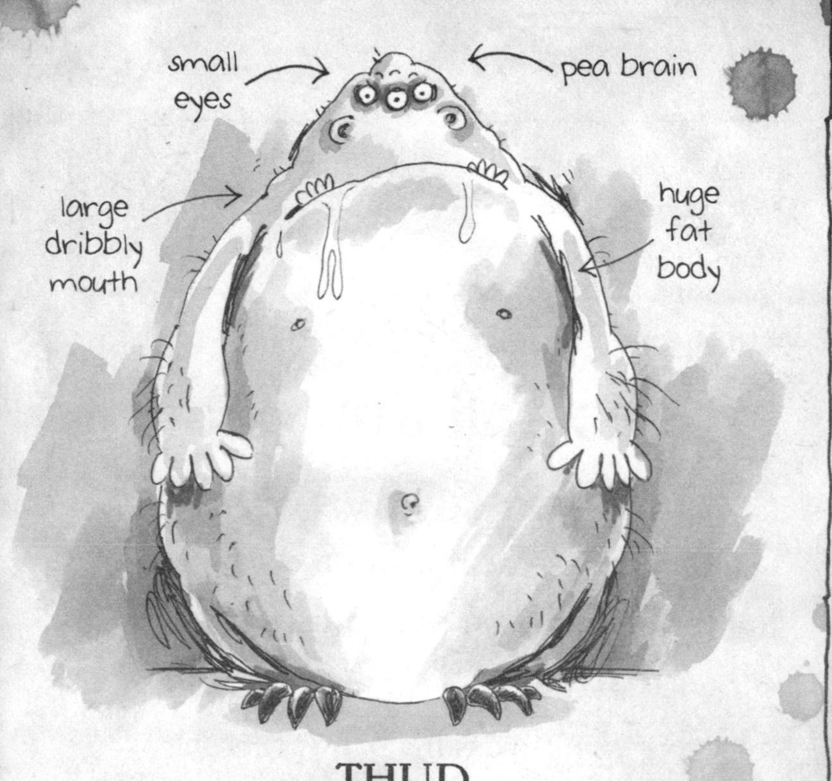

THUD

Thuds are large, dumb monsters made almost entirely from muscle and fat - and with a brain the size of a pea. Thuds can only perform one or two simple tasks and are so heavy they flatten anything they sit on - usually other monsters.

Thuds mostly hire themselves out as bouncers and bodyguards.

4

The Tall Jub Jub

'What's it doing?' asked Will, as the Thud shuffled over to Miffni and Pong Pong and held a long stick up to them. The creature stared at the stick for a long time with a large frown across his brow, then he grunted and ushered the pair inside.

'It's difficult to tell how old monsters are just by looking at them,' Urk explained. 'I think he was measuring them to see if they're *big* enough for The Monster Mash. Miffni is younger than me, but she can usually pass for a teenager

because she's so massive and Pong Pong is OK because Squidlets are so tall.'

'But that means we can't follow them,' said Will. 'We're both much shorter than the Thud's measuring stick.'

'You're right,' said Urk. 'But *together* we might just be tall enough.'

'Uh?' said Will, and then gasped when Urk ducked beneath his Jub Jub sack.

'Give me the forks and carry me on

your shoulders,' Urk's voice whispered from somewhere inside the dark tent of material. 'Then we should be about the same height as the stick!'

'And if we're not?' asked Will.

'Then the Thud will make us as flat as a pancake,' Urk swallowed.

After a short struggle and much tugging of material, Urk and Will eventually left the doorway and tottered across the road as one tall Jub Jub. Will could see very little through the thick, dark fabric and had to rely on Urk nudging with his hooves to guide him to The Monster Mash.

A tiny monster hopped up to the entrance in front of them and was immediately ushered inside after flashing his ID card at the Thud. But the bouncer

quickly barred the doors again as the
unsteady Jub Jub teetered to a halt.

'Good evening,' Urk said cheerily, waving a friendly fork.

'HMMMPH!' grunted the Thud, moving forward with his measuring device.

As the stick came closer, Urk's eyes widened when he saw that they needed a few extra centimetres to gain entry to the club, so he quickly sat up straight and craned his neck until his head drew level with the top.

'Fine weather we're having,' he gasped, as the creature frowned at the stick. 'Being such a *tall* teenager, I usually get to see it first as I'm so very high up. Not that we get a lot of weather here in Monsterland, being underground and all . . .'

Fortunately the Thud was using every ounce of brainpower to study the stick and paid no attention to Urk's nervous babbling. After what seemed like an eternity of concentration and a small amount of dribble, the creature arrived at a decision.

'YOU GO IN NOW,' grunted the Thud and nodded towards the door.

'Jolly good!' chirped Urk, and slumped with a sigh when the stick was taken away. He then gave Will a few light hoof-kicks to steer him towards the door, waving his forks for balance as they staggered into The Monster Mash.

5
Rumblefart

The Monster Mash was very noisy with thumping music and loud monster voices. Will didn't want to miss out on seeing a monster youth club so he tore a small hole in the Jub Jub sack to peep through.

The room was a large brown

dome filled with monsters dancing, monsters sitting around slurping slug-shakes and scoffing beetle-burgers, and a couple of small monsters who were kicking a ball of dung around the floor.

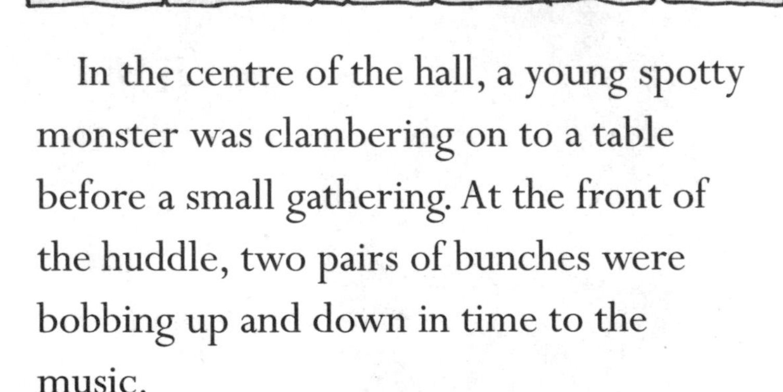

In the centre of the hall, a young spotty monster was clambering on to a table before a small gathering. At the front of the huddle, two pairs of bunches were bobbing up and down in time to the music.

'Over there!' yelled Urk, seeing Miffni and Pong Pong.

As the spotty monster mounted the table and cleared his throat, Will quickly shuffled forward and lurked at the back of the group. From there he could hear

what was going on and Urk could keep an eye on his sister and her friend.

On his tabletop podium, the spotty monster frowned at the Jub Jub.

'I see we have a new recruit!' he said, singling out the lurking Jub Jub. The smaller monsters glanced back at the tall, dark stranger so Urk waved a fork at them, grateful that Miffni and Pong Pong's attention remained fixed on the speaker.

'For those of you who don't already know, I am Rumblefart!' roared the monster, flicking up his feelers and raising his arms dramatically, causing Miffni and Pong Pong to squeal with excitement.

'Revolting leader of the Monster Mob and master of stinky bottom burps!'

'HONK! HONK!' cheered the group.

'The purpose of the Monster Mob is to perform mass scares to large groups of fleshblobs!' Rumblefart continued, unfolding the familiar poster advertising *Beauty and the Beast*. 'And our first performance is tomorrow night, where we will terrify the audience in this silly school play!'

'It's not just Miffni and Pong Pong,' Urk whispered urgently.

'So I hear,' whispered Will. 'We're up against a whole mob!'

'WHO'S TALKING?' Rumblefart demanded, squinting into the crowd.

The Monster Mob immediately turned and glared at the newcomer.

‘Er, I was just wondering what the plan was, exactly,’ said Urk in a gruff voice.

‘Well, if you had *bothered* to show up to our first meeting,’ sniffed Rumblefart, ‘you would know that we intend to take over the stage and deliver an evening of frights that the audience will never forget!’

'HONK! HONK!' the mob cheered excitedly.

'Oh,' said Urk, and then flinched when Will prodded him from under the sack. 'And what about the little fleshblobs who are already on the stage, what are you . . . I mean, what are *we* going to do to them?'

'If they get in your way you can do whatever you want,' Rumblefart replied coldly. 'The Monster Mob are rebels who ignore the scare rules of Monsterland. Which is why frightening grown-ups will be so much fun. They don't even *believe* in monsters, so it'll come as quite a shock when we appear on stage.'

'And how will we get into the school?' Urk asked, wondering if he was pushing his luck with too many questions. 'I mean it would be a shame to get all the way there to find the doors are locked.'

'Everything has already been arranged,' said Rumblefart, looking very pleased with himself as he addressed the rest of the mob. 'You see I have an undercover monster inside the school who feeds me all the information I need.'

'Grant Butcher!' gasped Will.

Urk quickly coughed into a fork to disguise his friend's voice, but the Monster Mob had already lost interest in the newcomer. They were now focused entirely on Rumblefart, who was demonstrating some of the many frights he had planned for the show.

'Are you sure this Grant Butcher is the insider?' whispered Urk.

Will thought about the school bully. He already knew about monsters wearing fleshblob suits to move around in the daytime and was annoyed that he hadn't spotted it sooner. Grant was the meanest kid in school, who lived to make other kids' lives a misery – and he'd taken to the role of the beast in the play a little too easily!

'I'm sure it's Grant Butcher,' said Will.

'Then we'll deal with him too,' whispered Urk, turning his attention back to the mob leader.

'. . . and as a grand finale I plan to blow the terrified audience off their chairs with the biggest, foulest fart ever witnessed!'

Rumblefart concluded, nodding graciously as the crowd whooped and clapped. 'But I will need two volunteers to bring Stinkypinks on the night to ensure the most revolting bouquet.'

Miffni and Pong Pong immediately put their hands up.

'Excellent,' said Rumblefart. 'The rest of you will meet me in the playground before curtain up at seven p.m. Then we will take to the stage and turn *Beauty and the Beast* into *Beauty and the Beastly Bottom*!' he yelled, turning his back on the crowd and letting out two honking farts that made Urk's forks vibrate.

'HONK! HONK!' cheered the Monster Mob.

As the smaller monsters drifted away in search of refreshments, Urk watched as Miffni and Pong Pong flustered around Rumblefart, who dismounted the table like a saggy beachball. Will was watching too, and after a hoof-nudge from his friend, the boy shuffled closer so they could eavesdrop.

'Oh, you were wonderful, Rumblebum!' sighed Pong Pong, batting her eyelids at the monster.

'His name is Rumble*fart*,' corrected Miffni, batting her own eyelids even harder.

The two monsters then stopped and glared at each other.

'Actually, you're both correct,' said

Rumblefart, slithering between the fuming friends. 'My name *is* Rumblefart,' he smiled, nodding to Miffni. 'And I *was* truly wonderful!' he added, patting Pong Pong on the head.

Miffni and Pong Pong immediately put their squabbling aside to take instructions from their leader. Rumblefart told them that a large crop of Stinkypinks could be found in Monsterland's Grisly Gardens and stressed how important the flowers were for the success of his grand finale.

The pair then hung on every word as the spotty monster went on to describe in detail how the revolting blooms guaranteed a belly full of wind that would smell like an open sewer.

'Anyone would think he's reading poetry to them,' whispered Will, as Miffni and Pong Pong swooned over fancy fart descriptions, including 'The putrid bum-rattler' and 'A stinky honkeroo'.

'They must have a serious crush on him!' whispered Urk. 'Which explains my sister's sudden interest in scaring fleshblobs.'

Urk and Will watched as Rumblefart finally handed two brown sacks to Miffni and Pong Pong, and then bounded away towards the exit of The Monster Mash – delivering a series of tooting farts with each hefty hop.

'He's so handsome!' sighed Miffni, clasping her hands together.

‘And gifted too,’ sighed Pong Pong, wafting a hand in front of her snout. ‘I believe his farts are the foulest thing I’ve ever smelled!’

The pair sniffed the air dreamily until the last traces of rotten cabbage were gone, then they skipped away arm in arm, swinging their empty sacks with glee.

As they left The Monster Mash and made their way towards Monsterland’s Grisly Gardens, Miffni and Pong Pong were too deep in their romantic daydreams to notice a tall, raggedy figure zigzagging after them.

6
The Grisly Gardens

When Miffni and Pong Pong entered the Grisly Gardens, the tall Jub Jub ducked behind a bush and emerged moments later as a small young monster and a *regular*-sized Jub Jub. Urk immediately took out the *Monsterbook* and looked up Rumblefart, informing Will that they were now up against a rebellious teenage Windbag.

WINDBAG

Windbags can appear fat or thin, depending on how much wind they have stored in their bellies. They can inflate up to three times their normal size on a diet of beans and cabbage - and shrivel down again when they expel their wind in the form of farts.

The farts smell like whatever Windbags eat and their bottoms can toot like a well-tuned trumpet.

'Yuck!' said Will, after reading the Windbag description.

'I know!' replied Urk, pulling a face. 'A diet of cabbage and beans!'

'So what's our plan now?' asked Will. 'Telling your parents about your sister won't do any good now we're dealing with Rumblefart and his Monster Mob. And Miffni and Pong Pong would probably warn him that we've been snooping around.'

'We also have the monster at your school to worry about,' said Urk.

'Grant Butcher,' sighed Will. 'If I'd known he was a monster, we could have dealt with him ages ago and Rumblefart would never have known about the school play.'

'We'll just have to come up with a

brand-new plan,' said Urk, peering over the bush as Miffni and Pong Pong strolled up to a Snot Tree, plucked Bogey Buds from its branches and stuffed them in their mouths. 'But in the meantime I think we should keep an eye on those two to see if they reveal any more information.'

SNOT TREES

Trees with a snotty sap that creates edible Bogey Buds on their branches.

Urk and Will followed at a safe distance as Miffni and Pong Pong made their way through the winding paths of the Grisly Gardens, examining all the strange flowers and shrubs that Monsterland had to offer.

GRISLY GARDENS

Grisly Gardens contains all known plants that thrive under Monsterland's murky lightbulbs, including:

VILE VINES

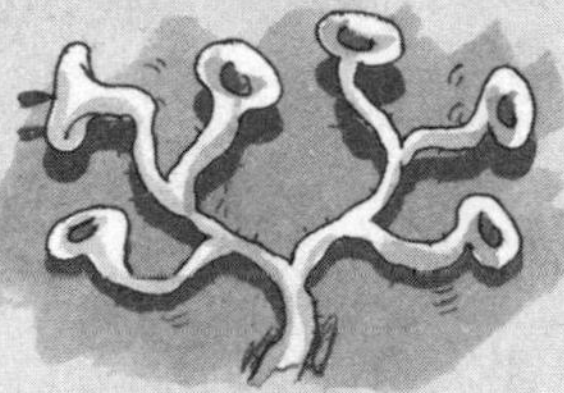

Vines that grab bare feet and suck on toe jam.

SINGING NETTLES

Poisonous nettles that lure their victims with a cheery song.

BURPING BUSH

A thick mossy bush with small burping buds.

TWO LIPS

Large flowers with big red mouths for eating bugs.

WARNING

Visitors to the Grisly Gardens may eat the fruits and flowers on display, but are warned that the fruits and flowers on display might try to eat them too!

Urk steered Will round the jabbing thorns of an aggressive shrub, then they hurried down the path and hid behind the thick, damp stalk of a giant mushroom. They poked their heads out and watched as Miffni and Pong Pong entered a large flowerbed filled with bright pink blooms.

'Those are roses!' whispered Will, pressing his forks either side of his nose as a revolting stench suddenly filled his nostrils. 'But I can't

smell them because there seems to be an open sewer nearby.'

'Those are Stinkypinks,' Urk chuckled. 'And what you're smelling is their putrid perfume.'

To confirm this, Miffni and Pong Pong began snatching off the heads of the flowers and stuffing handfuls of the bright pink petals into their sacks. They stomped through the bushes chatting and laughing, and by the time they were finished the flowerbed was bare.

Urk and Will pressed themselves close to the mushroom stalk as Miffni and Pong Pong stomped back along the path, too busy listing all the many wonders of Rumblefart to pay attention to the giant fungus. That was until they heard a very loud noise that stopped them in their tracks.

'ATCHOOOO!' sneezed Urk, and clasped his hands across his mouth.

Urk and Will didn't dare peek round the fungus stalk to see if they'd been spotted, so the next thing they saw was a long stripy tentacle that coiled round their waists and yanked them into the open.

Pong Pong suspended them effortlessly with her extendable limb as Miffni stepped forward and stood face to face with her brother, who was wriggling and kicking his legs wildly.

'Well, well, well!' she snorted. 'What are *you* doing here?'

'None of your business!' Urk growled, sounding braver than he felt.

'They followed us!' said Pong Pong, shaking the prisoners irritably.

'No! We just came here to see the Monster Muncher plant,' Urk said quickly. 'But then we saw you two picking flowers and thought we'd better stay out of your way. So we hid behind the giant mushroom.'

Miffni narrowed her eyes and turned to Will.

'Is that true?' she asked, prodding the Jub Jub with a chubby finger.

Will nodded eagerly, hoping Urk's sister wouldn't glance under his flapping sack to find a pair of muddy trainers.

dangling in the air. If Miffni discovered that her brother's friend was a fleshblob, the school play would be the least of their worries.

'What do you think, Pong Pong?' asked Miffni, scratching her chin thoughtfully.

'I think they're lying!' Pong Pong growled, and gave them another hard shake.

'But if they're telling the truth,

I wouldn't want to disappoint my darling little brother,' sneered Miffni, giving her friend a wicked grin. 'Maybe we should make sure they get a *really good look* at the Monster Muncher?'

'But they're annoying little Flea Bugs and we hate them,' frowned Pong Pong, scratching her head. 'Why would we want to help them if we hate them?'

'I mean we're going to dump them *in* the Monster Muncher, you pea-brain!'

snapped Miffni, rolling her eyes at her friend's stupidity as she stomped away.

'Bring them!' she demanded.

Pong Pong grudgingly followed Miffni, mumbling to herself as she dragged Urk and Will through a winding path of Creepy Creepers. Eventually they came to the Monster Muncher enclosure where the plant twitched with excitement as its roots detected a possible meal approaching.

Under Miffni's instructions, Pong Pong put down her sack of petals and dangled the prisoners over the open mouth of the Monster Muncher, where a large wet tongue lapped hungrily at the air.

'Any last words?' asked Miffni, peering up at them.

Will glanced down into the gaping mouth of the plant, but he was too terrified to speak and left it to Urk, trusting that his friend would say whatever was needed for his sister to set them free – even if it meant some serious begging and flattery.

'Lipgloss makes you look fat!' Urk hissed, folding his arms defiantly.

'Uh?' gasped Will.

With a nod from Miffni, Pong Pong suddenly released Urk and Will and

they dropped into the sticky, gaping mouth of the Monster Muncher plant.

Urk's sister and her friend then skipped away down the path, shrieking with laughter.

7
The Monster Muncher

'I thought you were going to flatter her or beg for mercy!' Will gasped, desperately trying to pull himself free from the thick, sticky goo that they were sitting in. 'And now we're going to get gobbled up by a giant daisy!'

'Miffni would have told Pong Pong to drop us in no matter what,' said Urk, pulling off his rucksack and placing it in his lap. 'But we won't be gobbled up,' he added reassuringly. 'We'll just be stuck here until tomorrow night when the gardeners will come and pull us out.'

'How do you know?' asked Will.

'Because she's thrown me in here before,' said Urk, pulling out the *Monsterbook* and flicking through the 'Putrid Plants and Foul Flowers' section. 'But I don't plan on staying that long.'

Will realized they were not actually sinking any further into the flower and relaxed a little as Urk found the Monster Muncher description and opened the book for them both to read.

MONSTER MUNCHER

Monsterland's largest flower will eat anything that strays into its sticky centre. It takes months for the gooey trap to melt down a whole monster, and its victims usually die of boredom long before that happens.

The Monster Muncher is very sensitive to strong flavours and will spit out anything that tastes unpleasant.

'I guess we both taste good,' said Will.

'It looks that way,' said Urk, glancing around until his eyes fell on something large and brown that was propped against the railings of the enclosure. 'But I'll bet *they* taste pretty unpleasant.'

He was looking at Pong Pong's sack of Stinkypinks.

'She must have forgotten to pick them up!' gasped Will.

Urk nodded and leaned forward as far as he could on the swaying stem of the flower, but the sack was just out of reach. Then he spotted Will's shiny cutlery and raised an eyebrow.

After a few minutes spent tying the forks together with loose threads from the Jub Jub cloth, they had a long crooked tool that would reach through the railings.

Luckily the sack was light, and after a few false starts they managed to drag it into the flower.

Once it was in reach of his hands, Urk passed the forks back to his friend and opened the top of the sack. His nose suddenly filled with putrid perfume and he quickly snatched it shut again.

'Yep! They should do the trick,' he gagged. 'Now hold your breath!'

Urk held his breath too as he shook the contents of the sack all around them and then watched with watering eyes as the Stinkypink petals began to sink into the goo. At first nothing happened, then the flower began twitching beneath them as it absorbed the foul flavours.

'Any minute now!' warned Urk.

Will nodded bravely and closed his eyes as the flower suddenly lurched backwards and then flung them across the Grisly Gardens in a shower of sticky pink petals.

Fortunately they landed in a shallow pond full of harmless Bogtoads, who snatched the petals with their long

tongues while the water washed away the goo.

'That was lucky,' said Urk, helping Will out of the pond and shaking the water from Pong Pong's empty sack. 'Any further and we would have landed in that cactus patch.'

'Very lucky!' agreed Will, eyeing a bed of tall sharp spines as he stooped to wring the bottom of his Jub Jub cloth.

The soggy pair quickly made their

way out of the Grisly Gardens, keeping an eye open for Miffni and Pong Pong as they headed back to the tunnels and the safety of Will's bedroom. They still had Rumblefart and the Monster Mob to deal with, and needed a safe place to come up with a brand-new plan.

After chomping their way through several bags of crisps and slurping down glasses of orange squash, Urk and Will

spent a long time studying the Windbag description in the *Monsterbook*. They were looking for anything they might have missed on how to defeat Rumblefart.

'All it mentions is farts!' said Will. 'And we already knew that.'

'He does seem to have a very talented bottom,' said Urk, drumming his fingers on the book. 'But I bet my sister and her

friend wouldn't be so keen on Rumblefart if he wasn't so foul.'

'They'll probably like him even more when he eats those Stinkypinks!' said Will, screwing his face up. 'But at least he'll only be eating one sack of petals instead of two, making his grand finale only half as revolting.'

'I wonder what his Monster Mob would think if he wasn't revolting at all?' Urk wondered aloud, pointing to the line describing how Windbag farts smell like whatever they eat. 'I mean, what if he turned up tomorrow night smelling of . . .'

The young monster racked his brain for something pretty and girly that looked like a Stinkypink.

'Roses!' gasped Will, grabbing the

empty sack and waving it in the air. 'We can fill this up with roses and switch it with Miffni's Stinkypinks! They look exactly the same and Rumblefart won't know the difference because he hasn't got a nose!'

'But where will we get roses at this time of night?' asked Urk.

Will smiled, tossing the sack over his shoulder. 'Follow me!'

Will led his friend silently past his parents' bedroom, down the dark stairs and out into the back garden. By the light of the moon, Urk's eyes widened when he saw dozens of bushes filled with bright pink flowers.

'My dad *loves* his roses,' whispered Will.

'They *really are* exactly like Stinkypinks!' Urk gasped, poking his large nostrils into one of the roses and smiling at the scent. 'But won't your dad notice they're missing?'

'I'm sure he won't miss a few,' said Will, knowing full well that his dad knew every flower and probably had names for them. 'And it's for a very good cause.'

The pair made short work of filling the sack with rose petals, leaving just enough flowers remaining on the bushes so Will's dad wouldn't be too upset. Then they tiptoed back up to the boy's bedroom to

finely tune the plan to turn the Monster Mob against Rumblefart.

They called it the Pong Plot and worked on it for most of the night.

8
The Pong Plot

On the opening night of *Beauty and the Beast*, the audience chattered cheerily as they took their seats in front of the stage in the school assembly hall. Behind the red curtain, Will had finished his technical preparations for the Pong Plot and was making sure his parents were not in their seats. He'd used every excuse he could think of to keep them away, and was relieved to see that it had worked.

'You're not in your costume!' shrieked a startled voice.

Will snatched the curtains back together and turned round to find Miss Star standing behind him, her arms loaded with a pile of tatty scripts. The drama teacher had been running around like a headless chicken for the past hour and judging by her untidy appearance, the school play was starting to take its toll.

'Er, I was just about to change,' said Will, and he was hurrying forward when the teacher dropped the scripts all over the floor and burst into tears. 'Are you OK, Miss Star?' he frowned, gathering up the sheets of paper.

'Oh, I just have a lot on my mind,' she gasped, mopping her eyes with a tissue.

Will had a lot on his mind too, and many things still to do before the Monster Mob arrived. Getting the drama teacher out of the way was one of them, but he had no idea how to do it.

'I can hand these out for you,' he offered, shuffling the scripts into a pile. But he stood up to see Miss Star sprinting down the corridor, sobbing loudly as she burst through the exit doors. 'The St Margaret's school play *finally* got the better of her,' Will sighed, and crossed the drama teacher off his mental list of things to do.

A nearby classroom had been turned into a changing room where the children were merrily pulling on their costumes. With all the hustle and bustle no one paid any attention as Will dumped the

scripts on a table, grabbed two foam tree costumes and hid them under the stage. He then legged it down the corridor to the school canteen where Urk would soon be arriving through a hidden doorway.

HIDDEN DOORWAY

Secret doorways where monsters can enter the world of fleshblobs without being seen.

Will poked his head through the double doors and looked around for his friend.

'Pssst!' said the large potted fern in the corner of the empty hall.

Still having no idea where the Monster Mob planned to enter the school, Will held his breath as the plant began to rustle. Then he sighed with relief as Urk stepped through the leaves and waved at him.

'How's it going?' asked the monster, trotting over to his friend.

'OK so far,' said Will, leading Urk back through the empty corridor. 'Luckily the drama teacher has fled the scene, but we still have to make sure my classmates are safe before Rumblefart and his Monster Mob arrive.'

'What about the undercover monster?' asked Urk.

'I've been watching Grant Butcher all afternoon,' said Will. 'But I lost track of him while I was setting up the stage. He's not in the changing room, which means he must have crept away to meet with the mob.'

'Well, I managed to swap the Stinkypink sack with the one filled with roses,' said Urk, blinking at the bright interior of the school. 'And Miffni and Pong Pong left early this evening to deliver them to Rumblefart.'

'What did you do with the *real* Stinkypink sack?' asked Will.

'I stuffed it under Miffni's bed.' Urk laughed. 'Her room is so smelly she won't even know they're there!'

As they approached the noisy changing room, Urk and Will pressed their backs against the wall and Will quickly poked

his head round the door. Miss Star hadn't returned and Grant was still nowhere to be seen, but all the other kids were present so he gave Urk the nod.

'Are you sure we can't just shut the door and lock it?' Urk whispered.

'We discussed this last night and decided it was too dangerous,' said Will, knowing this part of the Pong Plot would only work if his friend could be scary. 'Rumblefart's gassy bottom might start a fire!'

'So it's up to me to make sure they stay in there,' Urk sighed.

'I know you can do it,' said Will. 'Just pretend it's a play and *act* like you're terrifying.'

Urk counted to three and then leapt into the doorway waving his arms above

his head while Will stayed hidden and waited for the screams. When the screams didn't come and Urk's arms looked like they were getting tired, Will leaned sideways to speak to his friend.

'What's happening?' he whispered.

'Nothing,' said Urk, through the corner of his mouth. 'They're not even looking!'

'Then make some noise,' Will suggested. 'Growl at them.'

Urk cleared his throat with a series of short coughs and let out an almighty *ROAR!* The young monster was not very big or scary to look at, but he had an impressive pair of lungs that more than made up for it.

The chatter in the classroom halted abruptly and everyone turned their heads towards the noise. Upon seeing the monster their silence was quickly replaced with screams of terror, followed by the thunder of footsteps heading for the doorway – where Urk immediately froze.

'Flap your arms again!' Will gasped, as the stampede drew closer. 'Or they'll trample you to death!'

Urk quickly threw his arms around and added more growls and snarls for good measure. The kids that *had* intended to charge straight through him swiftly changed their minds and screeched to a halt, slamming the door to keep the monster out and tugging the blind across the window.

'Phew!' sighed Will. 'I thought I was going to have to scrape you off the floor!'

'Me too!' gasped Urk, feeling quite proud of himself when he heard desks and chairs being dragged in front of the door. 'Now let's hope *you* don't freeze like that when we get on stage!'

'Speaking of which, we'd better get

changed,' said Will, hurrying to the backstage area and pulling out the tree costumes. He sized them up and passed the smaller one to Urk. 'We can't risk Miffni recognizing you when the Monster Mob arrive!'

The two friends slipped into the foam tree trunks and shifted them around until they were peering through the eyeholes. It was now five minutes to seven, so they shuffled off to keep a lookout for Rumblefart.

The night before, Urk had studied a map of hidden doorways alongside Will's rough blueprint of the school and decided the rear entrance was the most likely place where the monsters would arrive – especially if Rumblefart had someone working on the inside. So the two trees took up positions either side of the corridor and waited.

While Will and Urk's sights were fixed on the rear doors of the school, they heard the flush of a toilet chain and the *bang* of another door behind them. This was followed by footsteps stomping along the corridor towards them.

The pair exchanged worried glances before shuffling round, and standing before them was a monster.

9

M-m-m-monsters!

The creature standing before Urk and Will was actually more of a beast than a monster. And it wasn't even a real beast because it had cardboard tubes for horns, large painted eyeballs and its teeth appeared to be made from egg boxes.

'What are you two doing?' Grant Butcher demanded, his face glaring out at them through the jaws of his mask. 'I heard screaming. Where is everyone?'

'They're safe,' said Will, stepping in front of the bully. 'And what are *you* doing

out here, as if I didn't already know!'

'That's none of your business, *Willow*!' Grant sneered, stepping up to Will and rolling up his sleeves. 'Now get out of my way or I'll give you something to weep about, *Willow*!'

'You're here to let them in and show them to the stage, aren't you?' said Will,

firmly standing his ground. 'I know everything, so you might as well admit it.'

'What are you talking about?' growled Grant. 'Get out of my way!'

The bully made a move to push Will over, when there was an almighty *BANG*

as the rear entrance doors burst open and the Monster Mob stormed down the corridor.

A bloated Rumblefart was up front bragging about a bellyful of Stinkypinks, closely followed by Miffni and Pong Pong, who were hanging on every word. The smaller monsters were straggling behind like ugly ducklings, shouting 'HONK! HONK!' in loud, rowdy voices.

'Them!' said Will, shuffling aside so Grant could see his friends.

'M-m-m-monsters,' burbled the cardboard beast.

Rumblefart stormed past the foam trees, thinking they were props and paused in front of Grant Butcher. The petrified boy stared up at the fuming Windbag, his real eyes almost as wide as the ones painted on his cardboard head.

'Is this meant to be scary?' Rumblefart asked, flicking one of the horns.

The boy was too terrified to speak so he nodded very slowly.

‘Well, it’s not!’ snorted Rumblefart, rearing up on his tentacles. ‘THIS IS SCARY!’ he roared, blasting the boy with a bone-rattling bellow that made the strips of paper hair flap angrily on his mask.

Urk and Will peered at each other over the heads of the smaller monsters and stifled a chuckle when Grant Butcher, who was obviously just a mean bully and not a monster at all, ran screaming down the corridor.

The Monster Mob roared with laughter and Rumblefart bowed graciously. 'That was the warm-up act!' chortled the Windbag. 'And now it's time for my big entrance!'

Urk and Will waited until Rumblefart and the Monster Mob bounded away towards the stage and then followed close behind, pausing like statues whenever the monsters glanced back.

'Did you bring the new script?' whispered Urk.

'Yep!' whispered Will, pulling his arm into the foam trunk. It reappeared moments later with several sheets of tatty paper covered in notes and scribbles where the new version of *Beauty and the Beast* had been edited to perfection.

'Are you nervous?' asked Urk.

'Yep!' sighed Will, as they crept towards the backstage area.

When they caught up with the mob, Rumblefart was bouncing up and down behind the red curtain, preparing for his big entrance. The audience obviously mistook his loud thumping for a drum roll because the assembly hall slowly fell silent.

The two trees quickly took their places either side of the stage, where Urk switched on the fairy-tale music and Will picked up the narrator's microphone. He had a lot more lines to deliver than 'RUSTLE! RUSTLE!' and took a very deep breath as Rumblefart burst through the curtain.

10

Beast and the Beauties

Rumblefart bounded on to the stage waving his arms and roaring at the top of his voice. The audience had been ready

to applaud the beginning of the play, but seeing the monster charging towards them, their mouths fell open and their hands froze mid-clap.

Urk looked over to his friend and nodded eagerly, urging him to read the first lines. Will stared at Urk, and then at Rumblefart, and finally at the seated parents – who seemed to be waiting for a reason not to run screaming from the building.

The success of the Pong Plot now rested on the boy's ability to convince the audience that they were watching a play, so he lifted the microphone and began reading aloud from the script.

'"Once upon a time there was a big revolting beast called Rumblefart,"' said Will, his voice filling the hall from the

speakers at the back. '"Rumblefart was very fat and spotty with weird feeler things stuck on his head – for this was a land of scary creatures and he was their king."'

Urk grabbed the paper crown from

the prop table and tossed it on to the monster's head. Luckily, Rumblefart didn't notice because he was too busy trying to work out where the voice was coming from and why no one was screaming. The monster peered into the stunned audience and scratched his bottom angrily.

'"Rumblefart's royal bottom was also very spotty,"' Will added quickly, hoping a joke would break the stunned silence of the crowd. '"Which made it very itchy, and the smelly old king scratched it all day long."'

At this point the uncertain audience finally allowed themselves to clap and laugh because the creature on the stage was *obviously* a couple of kids in a very clever costume – and the king's itchy bottom was pretty funny.

'"There were two beautiful princesses who both wanted to marry King Rumblefart,"' Will continued with relief, as Miffni and Pong Pong stomped on to the stage. '"Their names were Miffni and Pong Pong, and no one could decide who was the most beautiful."'

'Neither of them!' heckled Urk, making the crowd laugh even louder.

Confused by the audience's reaction and sensing something was wrong, Miffni and Pong Pong immediately hurried to the front of the stage to get instructions

from Rumblefart. But the Windbag ignored them as he belted out his scariest roars, which were quickly drowned out as the narrator's voice continued.

'"King Rumblefart couldn't decide which of the beautiful princesses he liked more,"' said Will, as the remaining Monster Mob entered the stage, jumping up and down and poking out their tongues. '"So he had a big party and invited every scary creature in the land."'

Urk quickly changed the music from fairy-tale to disco, which made the bouncing mob seem like they were dancing. The audience merrily clapped along in time to the song and chuckled at the strange little dancers.

'"At the party, smelly old Rumblefart planned to ask one of the princesses to become his queen,"' Will continued, watching as Miffni and Pong Pong now appeared to be following the story – glaring at each other as they wondered who would be chosen. '"And to decide which one, the king set them both a challenge."'

'ME! ME! ME!' yelled Pong Pong, getting carried away.

'YOU!' growled Miffni. 'DON'T MAKE ME LAUGH!'

By this time the smaller monsters in the Monster Mob had stopped jumping around and were watching the front of the stage, happy to put their scares on hold when it looked like a fight might break out.

'BUT *I'M* THE MOST BEAUTIFUL!' snapped Pong Pong.

'YOU'RE THE MOST *STUPID*!' snorted Miffni.

'I'M NOT STUPID!'

'YOU ARE TOO, AND SO IS *HE* IF HE DOESN'T PICK ME!'

Miffni and Pong Pong suddenly started grabbing at each other's hair-bunches, while Rumblefart continued

to work through his best scare routines, determined to get at least one scream from the crowd.

Unfortunately for the Windbag the audience were now thoroughly enjoying the play. They cheered and clapped and chuckled to themselves, marvelling at how much trouble the children had gone to with their wonderful costumes. And even though the story didn't make much sense, it was a lot of fun to watch.

Urk and Will were also watching the play very carefully.

They had written the script by guessing what the monsters would do when they arrived on stage – so the story would match the action and the audience would believe it was a play. So far it was working, but they still needed Rumblefart to deliver his grand finale on cue to pull the whole thing off.

'"The test King Rumblefart set for the princesses was to name his favourite flower,"' said Will, hoping Miffni and Pong Pong would fall for the bait and remind the Windbag of his gas-filled belly. '"And the one who could name it would become his queen and rule his scary kingdom."'

Miffni and Pong Pong paused in mid

hair-pull and racked their brains for the answer to the riddle – each believing that whoever answered correctly would be chosen by Rumblefart.

The audience hushed and Urk and Will held their breath.

'STINKYPINKS!' Miffni and Pong Pong yelled together.

At the mention of the foul blooms, Rumblefart, who was beginning to exhaust himself with so many different scare positions, suddenly remembered his grand finale. Grown-up fleshblobs were obviously immune to face frights and roars, but no one could ignore a beastly bottom-blast from a Windbag full of Stinkypinks!

'"When Miffni and Pong Pong gave their answer, King Rumblefart considered it very carefully,"' said Will, as Rumblefart turned his back on the audience and slowly bent over until his bottom was

high in the air. '"And he answered them in a very peculiar way . . ."'

HONK! HONK! HOOOOOONK! went the enormous fart, making the stage rattle and the curtain flap. It was also very long and loud as the Windbag squeezed out all of his gas, leaving the bloated monster looking like a shrivelled pear.

Rumblefart was very pleased with the tremendous fart volume, until he glanced back into the audience to find them not only still seated, but smiling with delight at the rosy scent and applauding the amazing special effects.

'"Rumblefart's favourite flowers were, of course, ROSES!"' said Will, as the pleasant perfume wafted back on to the stage, making the Monster Mob frown as it filled their nostrils. '"So the king didn't marry anyone and everyone went home."'

Urk and Will both crossed their fingers as the Monster Mob sniffed. The Pong Plot would only work if the monsters were disgusted by the sweet rosy scent, making them turn against their leader.

'YUCK!' they all gasped, gagging and screwing up their faces.

Miffni and Pong Pong were the first to leave. The fighting friends were

so appalled by the smell that they immediately went off Rumblefart, nudging the deflated Windbag aside as they stormed through the red curtain arm in arm. Then the smaller members of the Monster Mob quickly hurried after them, embarrassed and worried for their own scary status.

Urk and Will held their breath and watched the one remaining monster, wondering what would happen next. The Pong Plot had all gone according to plan, but they had no idea what the leader would do without his mob.

Abandoned by his followers, the saggy, baggy Rumblefart stood alone in the spotlight, looking angry and confused. But where an experienced adult monster might have pounced into the audience or wrecked the school – the teenage Windbag simply huffed away in a massive sulk, his bottom lip quivering as he fought the urge to bawl like a baby.

Urk quickly flicked on some jolly music and nodded to his friend.

'"And they all lived HAPPILY EVER AFTER!"' exclaimed Will.

11

Take a Bow

As the audience cheered and clapped and whistled, Urk and Will slipped backstage to make sure the monsters were all gone. Only when they were certain the coast was clear did they take off their tree costumes.

'I can't believe we just got away with that!' gasped Will.

'I know,' said Urk. 'Grown-ups *really* don't believe in monsters, huh?'

'Lucky for us!' said Will, and then frowned as something nagged at his

thoughts. 'But I've got a strange feeling we've forgotten something important.'

'The kids barricaded in the classroom?' Urk suggested, as they made their way down the corridor. 'You still have to find a way of convincing them to take credit for a school play they never even saw.'

'Yeah, maybe that's it,' said Will, and then stopped by a broom closet when he heard the sound of sobbing coming from inside. 'Someone's in there!' he whispered to Urk. 'Quick, you'd better hide!'

The young monster ducked into an alcove as Will lifted the latch and opened the door. Having no idea who or what he might find hiding inside, he did this very slowly and got ready to run.

'Miss Star!' he gasped, when he saw a familiar silhouette cowering in the darkness. But when the light flooded in from the corridor he noticed that his teacher's head wasn't exactly how he remembered it.

It was blobby and spotty, with two feelers drooping sadly.

'*You're* the undercover monster!' Will gasped, waving Urk out from his hiding place. 'I knew we'd forgotten something! It was the *true* identity of Rumblefart's insider!'

Urk and Will stood in the hallway as Miss Star stepped into the light, looking like a regular teacher from the neck down – but with the head of a thin, female Windbag. She was mopping her three eyes with a wad of soggy tissues.

'So you were in on it with Rumblefart!' said Urk.

'I didn't want to,' sobbed the monster teacher. 'He's my mean little brother who found out about the play by accident! Rumblefart threatened to tell everyone I was a horrible monster if I didn't help him, and I didn't want to leave the children . . .'

'So you left them to the Monster Mob instead?' accused Will.

'No!' she gasped. 'I was planning to stop him, but he must have suspected something because a big brute with hair-bunches ambushed me and shut me in the broom cupboard!'

'Tentacles or hooves?' asked Urk.

'Excuse me?' asked the teacher.

'Did she have tentacles or hooves?' Urk repeated.

'Er, I think she had hooves,' frowned Miss Star.

'That was Miffni,' Urk confessed. 'My mean little *sister.*'

'I've never heard of a monster living full-time as a human,' said Will, who had worked out that while other monsters used fleshblob suits to scare children, Miss Star was obviously using hers to educate them. And rather than being scary, she was one of his kindest teachers in the school.

'Oh, there are a few of us around,' said the Windbag, and then smiled as she looked back and forth between Urk and his fleshblob friend. 'Not *all* monsters want to be scary, as I'm sure you both already know.'

'Well, we got rid of Rumblefart for

you,' said Urk, quickly changing the subject. 'And I don't think he'll be trying anything again, not without his Monster Mob.'

'How did you do it?' asked Miss Star, and seeing the strange look her student was giving her, she quickly pulled on her fleshblob mask and tidied her hair.

'There isn't time to explain,' said Will, feeling more comfortable talking to his teacher with a human head. 'All you need to know is that the parents saw a great show, with some very clever costumes and a bit of a rubbish ending.'

'And the children?' gasped Miss Star.

'They've locked themselves in the changing room,' said Will, scratching his head. 'Do you think you can get them all on the stage to take a bow, and maybe tell them that it was Grant Butcher who scared them?'

'Yes, of course,' said the teacher. 'And where's Grant Butcher?'

'You'll probably have to search for him,' said Urk. 'He ran off when he saw your brother.'

'Oh dear,' said Miss Star, and then

pulled her shoulders back and straightened her jacket. 'It looks like I have a lot of very inventive explaining to do.'

Urk and Will nodded, and then left Miss Star to begin tying up the loose ends of the Pong Plot. As they proceeded towards the hidden doorway in the canteen,

Urk reassured Will that a monster living full-time as a fleshblob would have to be pretty good at thinking on her feet.

12

An Evening of Entertainment

'BOO!' said Urk, jumping from the wardrobe and dumping his rucksack on the floor. The young monster then collapsed in the beanbag next to his friend. After two evenings spent working on the Rumblefart case, he was looking forward to catching up on some TV.

'ARGH!' said Will. 'What's up?'

'My sister is staying at Pong Pong's for a whole week!' Urk grinned.

'So they're not chasing after Rumblefart any more?' asked Will.

'No,' said Urk. 'They've gone back to having very long conversations about different flavours of lipgloss.'

'Any sign of the teenage Windbag?' asked Will.

'No. I think he's probably gone into

hiding out of total embarrassment,' laughed Urk, and then suddenly remembered the second Windbag. 'But what about his sister? How did Miss Star get on after I left?'

'My classmates thought they'd be in trouble for missing the school play, and that their parents would be disappointed,' said Will. 'But Miss Star whisked them on to the stage in time for a standing ovation, and afterwards I helped her track down Grant Butcher.'

'Where was he?' asked Urk.

'Hiding in a tree!' laughed Will, remembering the cardboard head peeping out from the branches. 'Miss Star managed to coax him down, once she convinced him that there're no such things as monsters.'

'If only he knew!' laughed Urk. 'And Miss Star got to keep her job?'

'Even better,' said Will, reaching down the back of his beanbag and pulling out the evening paper. 'She got such a rave review for *Beauty and the Beast* that the school made her head of the drama department.'

THE EVENING NEWS

STAGE FRIGHT!

Scary version of *Beauty and the Beast* is a hit!

St Margaret's Elementary's school play was very popular with the audience. The story was quite short, but parents said it was hilarious and the costumes were AMAZING!

"Our drama teacher, Miss Star, gave the familiar fairy tale an exciting new spin and we are very lucky to have her at our school." said the Head Teacher.

(full story on page 7)

MISS STAR IS A STAR!

Teacher receiving bunch of roses.

'So I guess plays can be fun after all,' said Will.

'Yeah,' said Urk, grabbing a bag of crisps and pouring out two glasses of orange squash. 'But I'd still rather watch TV!'

'Me too,' agreed Will, with a chocolate bar in one hand and the remote control in the other. 'It's a lot less trouble!' he sighed, as they both flopped back for a quiet evening in.